# ROLL ALONG
## *Poems on Wheels*

· · · · · · · · · · · · · · · · · · · · · · · · · · · · · · · · · · · · · · · · · · · · · · · · · · · · · · · · · · · ·

## For Josh and Jonas
## and their Big Wheels

Margaret K. McElderry Books
Macmillan Publishing Company
866 Third Avenue
New York, NY 10022

Maxwell Macmillan Canada, Inc.
1200 Eglinton Avenue East
Suite 200
Don Mills, Ontario M3C 3N1

Macmillan Publishing Company is part of the Maxwell Communication Group of Companies.
First edition
Printed in the United States of America
10  9  8  7  6  5  4  3  2  1
The text of this book is set in Zapf International Medium.

Library of Congress Cataloging-in-Publication Data
Livingston, Myra Cohn.      Roll along : poems on wheels / Myra Cohn Livingston. — 1st ed.
            p.      cm.
        Summary: An anthology of contemporary poems by a variety of authors about wheels and vehicles that roll.
        ISBN 0-689-50585-X
        1. Children's poetry, American.   2. Transportation—Juvenile poetry.   3. Wheels—Juvenile poetry. [1. Transportation—Poetry.   2. Vehicles—Poetry.   3. Wheels—Poetry.   4. American poetry—Collections.]      I. Title.
        PS3562.I945R64   1993      811'.54—dc20                                      92-32714

# Roll Along
## *Poems on Wheels*

Selected by

MYRA COHN LIVINGSTON

MARGARET K. McELDERRY BOOKS
*New York*

Maxwell Macmillan Canada
*Toronto*

Maxwell Macmillan International
*New York   Oxford   Singapore   Sydney*

# Acknowledgments

•••••••••••••••••••••••••••••••••••••••••••••••••••••••••••

The editor and publisher thank the following for permission to reprint the copyrighted material listed below. Every effort has been made to locate all persons having any rights or interests in the material published here. Any existing rights not here acknowledged will, if the editor or publisher is notified, be duly acknowledged in future editions of this book.

Aitken & Stone Limited for "Esmé on Her Brother's Bicycle" and "School Buses" by Russell Hoban, from *The Pedaling Man* by Russell Hoban. Copyright © 1968 by Russell Hoban.

Curtis Brown Ltd. for "Making Work for Father," from *The Phantom Ice Cream Man* by X. J. Kennedy. Copyright © 1979 by X. J. Kennedy. Reprinted by permission of Curtis Brown Ltd.

The Ciardi family for "The Army Horse and the Army Jeep," from *The Reason for The Pelican* by John Ciardi, J. P. Lippincott. Copyright © 1959 by John Ciardi.

Doubleday for "Taxis," from *Taxis and Toadstools* by Rachel Field, copyright © 1926 by Doubleday, a division of Bantam Doubleday Dell Publishing Group, Inc. Used by permission of Bantam Doubleday Dell Publishing Group, Inc.

Estate of Norma Millay Ellis for "Travel" by Edna St. Vincent Millay. From *Collected Poems*, HarperCollins. Copyright © 1921, 1948 by Edna St. Vincent Millay. Reprinted by permission of Elizabeth Barnett, literary executor.

Farrar, Straus & Giroux, Inc., for "Jittery Jim," from *Laughing Time* by William Jay Smith. Copyright © 1990 by William Jay Smith. Reprinted by permission of Farrar, Straus & Giroux, Inc.

Kristine O'Connell George for "Double Wide." Copyright © 1993 by Kristine O'Connell George.

Harcourt Brace Jovanovich, Inc., for "The Train Melody," from *Everything Glistens and Everything Sings: New and Selected Poems*, copyright © 1987 by Charlotte Zolotow, reprinted by permission of Harcourt Brace Jovanovich, Inc.

HarperCollins Publishers for "The Gold-Tinted Dragon," from *Dogs & Dragons, Trees & Dreams* by Karla Kuskin. Copyright © 1980 by Karla Kuskin. Reprinted by permission of HarperCollins Publishers.

David Higham Associates for "I Love My Darling Tractor," from *Early in the Morning* by Charles Causley.

X. J. Kennedy for "My Mother Drives the Mailtruck," copyright © 1993 by X. J. Kennedy.

Karla Kuskin for "Dinos" and "The Ice Cream Truck," copyright © 1993 by Karla Kuskin.

Claudia Lewis for "Digging Machines at Work in the City," copyright © 1993 by Claudia Lewis.

J. Patrick Lewis for "The Auto-Eater," "Fire Engine," and "Hey, Taxi," copyright © 1993 by J. Patrick Lewis.

# CONTENTS

......................................................................

# 1·
# BICYCLES, SKATEBOARDS
## ······&·····························································
# ROLLER SKATES

## Bike Ride

Look at us!

We ride a
road
the sun has paved with
shadows.

We glide
on leaf lace
across tree spires
over
shadow ropes
of droopy wires.

We roll
through a shade tunnel
into light.

Look!
Our bikes
spin
black-and-white
shadow
pinwheels.

*Lilian Moore*

## Esmé on Her Brother's Bicycle

One foot on, one foot pushing, Esmé starting off beside
Wheels too tall to mount astride,
Swings the off leg forward featly,
Clears the high bar nimbly, neatly,
With a concentrated frown
Bears the upper pedal down
As the lower rises, then
Brings her whole weight round again,
Leaning forward, gripping tight,
With her knuckles showing white,
Down the road goes, fast and small,
Never sitting down at all.

*Russell Hoban*

Got a balloonloonloonloon
tied tight
to the wheeleeleeleel
of my bike,

If it broke
with a poke
got a speechless
old spoke.

*Judith W. Steinbergh*

# Making Work for Father

To hit a bump is what I like
So Father has to fix my bike.

Both handlebars a total wreck,
I wear the pedals round my neck.

Then Father, in an awful tizzy,
Swings the hound round till they both drop dizzy,

Scowls at my owl,
Growls at my mink,
Bites a big hole through the kitchen sink,
Kicks kindling wood from his workbenches,

And goes and gets his monkey wrenches.

*X. J. Kennedy*

## On Our Bikes

The roads to the beach
           are winding
  we glide down
         breeze-whipped
curving
      past hills of sand
  pedal and coast
         through wide smell of the sea
          old familiar sunfeel
  windwallop.

Race you to the water's edge!

*Lillian Morrison*

# I Am an Alley Skipper

slooping down
(avoiding glass and gravel)
on my bike
I beat the garbage men
to their Saturday haul:
cobbing the busted suitcase,
tacking to that plastic dish,
rescuing a desk drawer set adrift

I salvage
like a sea captain

until with treasures
piled high
in my wicker bike basket
I pedal
heavily home
still acting as look-out
scanning the alley
for any swag or loot
ready to "heave to"
on my mizzenmasted bike

*Cynthia Pederson*

## On a Bike

A curve came winding in the road
To make me stop.
I eased the brakes
To slow
    just where the city makes
    its pattern in the earth below.

The eucalyptus leaves blew clean.
I held my breath.
A dusty toad
Bulged gray
    and bulbous in the road.
    Then, next, a darting blue of jay

Streaked past the moment where I stood
In world so blue.
A pile of leaves
Lay dead
    until a crazy breeze
    stirred up the dusty road ahead

And there was someone in a car
Came roaring by.
He slammed his brakes
And cursed
    and asked the road to take.
    "This is the worst

Old mountain road!" he yelled.
The dust flew up.
He started down
The road.
    I watched him head to town
    and looked again to find the toad

And jay. But they had gone.
The place was dry,
All out of tune
And brown.
    "Why waste the whole good afternoon
    up here?" I asked myself, and hurried down.

*Myra Cohn Livingston*

# Nine Mice

Nine mice on tiny tricycles
went riding on the ice,
they rode in spite of warning signs,
they rode despite advice.

The signs were right, the ice was thin,
in half a trice, the mice fell in,
and from their chins down to the toes,
those mice entirely froze.

Nine mindless mice, who paid the price,
are thawing slowly by the ice,
still sitting on their tricycles
. . . nine white and shiny *micicles*!

*Jack Prelutsky*

today was spring
and yesterday's snow turned puddles
I broke my bike
from its cocoon
and hosed it down
and told the gas-station man
to put in 30 pounds
and rode to the park
but the park was brown
and the buds were brown
and the leaves that covered the ground
were brown
and the picnic tables
were upside down
I guess it hadn't heard yet
but there was one thing . . .
the kite caught up in the tree
was green

*Judith W. Steinbergh*

# The Sidewalk Racer
## or
# On the Skateboard

Skimming
an asphalt sea
I swerve, I curve, I
sway; I speed to whirring
sound an inch above the
ground; I'm the sailor
and the sail, I'm the
driver and the wheel
I'm the one and only
single engine
human auto
mobile.

*Lillian Morrison*

## 74th Street

Hey, this little kid gets roller skates.
She puts them on.
She stands up and almost
flops over backwards.
She sticks out a foot like
she's going somewhere and
falls down and
smacks her hand. She
grabs hold of a step to get up and
sticks out the other foot and
slides about six inches and
falls and
skins her knee.

And then, you know what?

She brushes off the dirt and the
blood and puts some
spit on it and then
sticks out the other foot

*again.*

*Myra Cohn Livingston*

# Unicycle

If you're climbing
a guywire
skyward,
right
to a high-wire
tightrope
out of sight,

The type
of cycle
for any guy
or girl
to try
is not a bi-

But a
U-
N-
I-

*John Ridland*

# 2.
# BUSES, TAXIS
## ·····&·····
# MOTORCYCLES

## *School Buses*

You'd think that by the end of June they'd take themselves
Away, get out of sight—but no, they don't; they
Don't at all. You see them waiting through
July in clumps of sumac near the railroad, or
Behind a service station, watching, always watching for a
Child who's let go of summer's hand and strayed. I have
Seen them hunting on the roads of August—empty buses
Scanning woods and ponds with rows of empty eyes. This
  morning
I saw five of them, parked like a week of
Schooldays, smiling slow in orange paint and
Smirking with their mirrors in the sun—
But summer isn't done! Not yet!

*Russell Hoban*

# Sleepy Schoolbus

Weekends, the battered yellow bus
   That calls at all our houses
And honks its horn to hurry us
   Draws shut its doors and drowses

Till, roused by Monday lunchbox smells,
   It yawns and reappears.
You look all worn out, yellow bus.
   Go home. Doze ten more years.

*X. J. Kennedy*

# *A Driver from Deering*

A school bus driver from Deering
disconcertingly kept disappearing:
he would head for Cape May,
but end up in Bombay
—because something was wrong with the steering.

*N. M. Bodecker*

# *Jittery Jim*

There's room in the bus
For the two of us,
But not for Jittery Jim.

He has a train
And a rocket plane,
He has a seal
That can bark and swim,
And a centipede
With wiggly legs,
And an ostrich
Sitting on ostrich eggs,
And crawfish
Floating in oily kegs!

There's room in the bus
For the two of us,
But we'll shut the door on *him*!

*William Jay Smith*

# Bussssssssssssssssss

Brakessssshisssssss
wheelsssssssssqueal
bussssssssssssssssss
ssssssssssssssto-ops.

Step in!   Step up!
the doors shut
the coins clink
the driver gives a friendly wink

She presses down the fat gas pedal
a creepy sound of scraping metal
the bus roars
an old man snores

Brakessssshissssssss
wheelsssssssssqueal
bussssssssssssssssss
ssssssssssssssto-ops.

Step down!   Step off!
Bus breathes.
Bussssssssssssssssss
leaves.

*April Halprin Wayland*

# The One I Always Get

And I step on the bus
And I put my money in the glass box
And I find a seat in back
    (it's better for jiggling)
And old women don't sit there
    (it's better for watching)
And you don't get squished.

And we speed up going down Wilshire
    (when people aren't waiting at bus stops)
And this driver, the one I always get, shrugs
    (when he's through counting transfers and
    winding up his money box)
And looks at me when he's pulling up at
    La Brea:

"Well," he says, "time for you to get off and
    get to your homework."
"Well," I say, looking back with my left eye
    and swinging around the pole and
    stepping down to the door,

"Well," I say, "see you tomorrow same
    as always."

            "Same as always," he mumbles
And swings the wheel to the curb,
And I jump off.

*Myra Cohn Livingston*

## Hey, Taxi

The meter ticks,
  The heater purrs,
The cabbie hums.
  His passengers?

Four boys who watched
  The Yankees win,
Have hailed a cab
  And piled in.

The city slows
  On baseball nights.
And when they stop
  For traffic lights,

The boys tune in
  To so-and-so,
Some rock band on
  The radio,

And just to show
  That *he* can squawk,
The cabbie sings
  *New Yawk, New Yawk.*

*J. Patrick Lewis*

# Taxis

Ho, for taxis green or blue,
   Hi, for taxis red,
They roll along the Avenue
   Like spools of colored thread!

> *Jack-o'-lantern yellow,*
> *Orange as the moon,*
> *Greener than the greenest grass*
> *Ever grew in June.*
> *Gayly striped or checked in squares,*
> *Wheels that twinkle bright,*
> *Don't you think that taxis make*
> *A very pleasant sight?*
> *Taxis shiny in the rain,*
> *Scudding through the snow,*
> *Taxis flashing back the sun*
> *Waiting in a row.*

Ho, for taxis red and green,
   Hi, for taxis blue,
I wouldn't be a private car
   In sober black, would you?

*Rachel Field*

## Taxi to the Airport

Meter clicking
Watch ticking
Racing down the street.

Taking curves
Jiggling nerves
Bouncing on the seat.

Heart thumping
Pulse pumping
Got a plane to meet.

*Marni McGee*

## Riding to School

"Hop on!" Dad said. He swooped me up.
I was there behind him in one jump.
"Put your hands in my pockets," he said. "Hold tight.
Don't be afraid. You'll be all right."

The motor snorted. It growled. In a roar
We were off, and I couldn't hear any more.
We whizzed past houses, the houses blurred.
We stopped at a light, the motor whirred.

"Hold on now, honey," Daddy said.
A roar again. We zoomed ahead.
The wind rushed by, it blew my hair.
I loved the brush of the rushing air.

Then we turned a corner and leaned to one side.
I was so scared I almost cried.
I pressed my cheek on the back of Dad's shirt
And shut my eyes till my eyelids hurt.

Suddenly Dad said, "We're there!"
He kissed me good-by. I ran up the stair.
I'd come to school as no one else had,
On a motorcycle with my dad.

*Martha Robinson*

# Riddle

In the dripping gloom I see
A creature with broad antlers,
Motionless. It turns its head;
One gleaming eye devours the dark.
I hear it cough and clear its throat;
Then, with a hungry roar, it charges into the night
And is swallowed whole.

*Ian Serraillier*

Motorcycle

# 3.
# *TRUCKS,*
# *TRACTORS, RIGS*
## ·····*&*··········································································
# *WAGONS*

# Traffic Rule I

One traffic rule
we all obey:
*the Mack truck has
the right of way.*

N. M. Bodecker

# My Mother Drives the Mailtruck

My mother drives the mailtruck
   That meets the morning train.
It drops its tailgate, takes on sacks
   Like big gray bags of grain.

It's starred and striped red white and blue—
   Six cylinders it fires—
As square-shaped as a can of glue
   That rolls on rubber tires.

Mom grits her teeth, tromps gas, and shoves
   The shift-stick—off we lurch.
Atop a bale of fourth class mail
   Up next to her I perch.

Down dusty country roads we cruise—
   You can't hear for the roar.
We rush, because folks craving news
   Jam-pack Jim's General Store.

Then home we head. The roads are squirreled
   And roostered, so we slow,
And me, I'm part of all the world
   Where letters come and go.

*X. J. Kennedy*

# Truck Quake

I can tell by trembles
when a truck roars past
when the backyard rumbles
from its many wheels
I don't need to run to the street to see . . .

when a truck roars past
I know how it feels.

*April Halprin Wayland*

## *Cacophony*

Garbage truck
sings its song:

"Mash, smash,
grink, chong,

goopidy guck,
grabbid slee,

garrup garruck,
pfoo skree
          *bluck.*"

*Eve Merriam*

# *Truckers*

I rigged a trailer behind my bike—
really a wagon, but I always like
to say "trailer," and "rig," like the truckers do,
and pretend I'm driving a big rig, too.

Then a real truck with a lumber load
on a flatbed trailer came down the road
big as a mountain, with a diesel stack
and eighteen wheels and a flag in back.

It slowed way down as it rumbled by
and the driver leaned out from way up high—
we gave each other the thumbs-up sign:
I liked his truck; he liked mine.

*Alice Schertle*

**34**

## Crane Dream

On an evening walk near a pond
my father pointed out a crane,
a gray-white bird like a spider
on stilts at the edge of a mirror.
As we strolled near, it flapped away
trailing long legs.

Once when I had a bad cold and stayed
home from school, I watched a crane
made of orange steel. The operator
sat in a glass box hung below the arm;
wispy cables and wheels, concrete blocks
and motors completed the machine.

By moving levers, the crane man could
slowly turn the arm, lower a cable,
pick up great pieces of steel or buckets
of concrete, then lower them gently
over a form or wall. One time he waved back
when I waved at him.

My friends say they'll drive taxis
or buses; Mickey says he'll fly
like his father and wear a uniform.
My parents see me study, murmur "Doctor"
or "Lawyer." Who knows? But I think
I'll climb into that box and run the crane.

*Jim Thomas*

## Digging Machines
## at Work in the City

Gawky, awkward,
arm joints bolted, bent,
the two—
huge yellow fellow
and partner, blue
with gangly trunk

scrape, sputter,
twist with groaning,
lift, swing back—

A ballet
for today
on the torn-up block.

*Claudia Lewis*

## *A Crusty Mechanic*

There was an old crusty mechanic
whose manners were fierce and tyrannic:
dull headlights would glare
at his furious stare,
—and dead engines turn over in panic!

*N. M. Bodecker*

## *Double Wide*

........................................................

Long load      Wide load

Side by side
Double wide
Slow load.

Left half      Right half

Sawed in half
Double wide
Lumbers past.

Mobile home
Going home.

*Kristine O'Connell George*

# *The Ice Cream Truck*

Shortly after six o'clock
across the street
and down the block,
sweet, insistent,
loud and clear
a nightly bell beguiles my ear.

Just yesterday I had this dream.
The ice cream truck
was pure ice cream.
The wheels were chocolate,
pretty nice,
the fenders all were orange ice.
The bumpers: mint.
The doors: pure peach.
A coffee handle opened each.
The roof,
which was pistachio,
looked very much like pale green snow
with bits of nuts.
The headlights shone
from deep within two sugar cones.
And in this dream I could not budge
but stood
unmoving
stunned by fudge.

When suddenly
way down the street
I heard the rush of running feet,
countless children, all those eyes
(every color
any size)
wide with hunger
and surprise.
Alerted by the bell's sweet tune
they ran,
and each child held a spoon.

*Karla Kuskin*

# Fire Engine

Up out of bed
   They hit the hole,
Ten firemen sliding
   Down the pole,

Then climb aboard
   The big machine,
The reddest red
   You've ever seen.

The siren screams,
   The engine roars.
Some people watch,
   From open doors,

A rainbow arc
   Across the lawn.
The chief keeps shouting,
   "Pour it on!"

The faithful statue's
   Standing by—
A spotted dog
   With one black eye.

*J. Patrick Lewis*

## *Learning to Drive the Tractor*

I kept after Dad, kept saying, "Let me drive."
So one Saturday when I was ten, a bright
day of sun, Dad said, "Climb up there," pointed
to the cold tractor seat. We went through gears
and clutch, how to start and stop; then he told
me to put it in neutral and turn the key.

Blissful! The tractor roared into life.
I followed directions and backed out
into the lot, turned and drove to a wagon.
Dad hooked it up, got on, and I drove away.
It was a long way to the ground; my knuckles
showed white on the wheel, but I got us to work.

We piled the wagon with oak and hickory,
loaded the saw and tools; again I started
the engine, let the clutch out smoothly,
brought us out of the woods, down the hill, across
the creek, up to the woodpile to unload.
I was so proud I grinned like the August sun.

Work done, again I made the motor roar
and turned into the shed and could not stop
and reached and reached for the brake and struck

the back wall so hard a wheel cracked off.
Dad flipped the key. Scared, I jumped down, screamed

"I wish
I were dead!"   "Whoa," said Dad, "nobody's hurt."

*Jim Thomas*

# I Love My Darling Tractor

I love my darling tractor,
I love its merry din,
Its muscles made of iron and steel,
Its red and yellow skin.

I love to watch its wheels go round
However hard the day,
And from its bed inside the shed
It never thinks to stray.

It saves my arm, it saves my leg,
It saves my back from toil,
And it's merry as a skink when I give it a drink
Of water and diesel oil.

I love my darling tractor
As you can clearly see,
And so, the jolly farmer said,
Would you if you were me.

*Charles Causley*

# The Gold-Tinted Dragon

What's the good of a wagon
Without any dragon
To pull you for mile after mile?
An elegant lean one
A gold-tinted green one
Wearing a dragonly smile.
You'll sweep down the valleys
You'll sail up the hills
Your dragon will shine in the sun
And as you rush by
The people will cry
"I wish that my wagon had one!"

*Karla Kuskin*

# 4·
# CARS, JEEPS
## ····· & ·······································································
# THE OPEN ROAD

# A Person of Ealing

A certain young person of Ealing
delighted in automobiling,
till someone named Hall
drove *him* up the wall,
—and parked him under the ceiling.

*N. M. Bodecker*

# Central Park Tourney

Cars
In the Park
With long spear lights
Ride at each other
Like armored knights;
Rush,
Miss the mark,
Pierce the dark,
Dash by!
Another two
Try.

Staged
In the Park
From dusk
To dawn,
The tourney goes on:
Rush,
Miss the mark,
Pierce the dark,
Dash by!
Another two
Try.

*Mildred Weston*

## *Car Wash*

Car,
   I give you over to
   the broad flapping fingers of a
   mechanical genie,
   squeezing soap on your head,
   wooshing wax in your eyes,
   blowing air on your sides,
   brushing your bottom,
   guiding you through a white house
   and out again, on roaring tracks,
   to a little man in orange,
   wiping off your face.

Car,
   what a surprise!
   how good to see you again
   shining, gleaming.

*Myra Cohn Livingston*

# Auto Body Shop

I watch the wrecks come in on the wreckers,
   ease down slowly in the bays,
I estimate the damage,
   compare it to what the owner says,
I watch when Willard's welding,
   making sparks like the Fourth of July,
and John's lying under the chassis
   muttering and soldering pipes.
I like when they spray paint the metal
   and it glows deep as a lake,
then the chrome and the bumpers and hub caps,
   Willard never makes a mistake.
When it's dry, I rub the fender,
   I wait till the guys go to eat,
I'm going to work in a body shop
   making broken cars new and sleek.

*Judith W. Steinbergh*

# The Auto-Eater

Once there was a noisy green
Compacto-Tracto-Car machine

That filled its rumbling stomach full
Of Cadillac convertible.

It ate a yellow taxicab
That came out looking like a slab,

And bit into a rusty heap
That used to be somebody's Jeep,

And mangled something from Japan
Into a *mini* mini–van.

One by one it chewed them all
And made them very *very* small.

*J. Patrick Lewis*

# *Automobile*

After toiling
Over the roads
All day on
Tired rubber wheels,

It cools its
Heels in the
Driveway, resting
Its metal, smiling.

*Valerie Worth*

# The Army Horse and the Army Jeep

"Where do you go when you go to sleep?"
Said the Army Horse to the Army Jeep.
"Do you dream of pastures beside a creek
With meadow grass to make you sleek?
Do you dream of oats and straw in a stall
And never a load in the world to haul?
Do you dream of jumping over the wall
To get at the apples that fall in the Fall?
Do you dream of haystacks steeple-tall?
Or what do you dream if you dream at all?"

> "Rrrrrrrrrr," said the Jeep
> And "Chug!"

"I dream of being greased for a week
On the Happy Rack by Gasoline Creek
In the Happy Garage where there's never a squeak,
But lakes of oil so black and sleek,
And Spark Plug Bushes, and no valves leak.
That's where I go when I go to sleep,"
To the Army Horse said the Army Jeep.

> And "Rrrrrrrrrr," said the Jeep
> And "Aaaaaaaaaa!"

*John Ciardi*

# *Dinos*

Stegosaurus
trampled grasses.
Tyrannosaurus
shook the trees.
And the mighty Brontosaurus
shivered prehistoric seas.
Then they were enormous.
Then they were tremendous.
Now they are enormous.
Now they are stupendous,
eating up the countryside
zooming far
varooming wide
streaking down a thousand highways
spilling smoke across the skyways
scattering the smallmobiles,
endless dinosaurs
on wheels.

*Karla Kuskin*

# *Freeway*

The man in the red Ferrari
Zoomed around us
Like we weren't moving.
He just took off,
Gave it the gas,
Practically left us sitting there
On the freeway. And don't you think my
Dad didn't give him a dirty look and
Mumble something about those darned
Little cars.
And
What's wrong with just going normal
Like you're supposed to
At sixty-five mph?

*Myra Cohn Livingston*

## Night Ride

The man in the moon
is shrouded in smog.
Smoke gets in his eyes.

Red taillights
down the highway
are sluggish fireflies.

Drivers grip
their steering wheels
as if mesmerized

inching through
the car jam
with honks and muffled cries.

*Lillian Morrison*

# Drivers
## or
## After Listening to Radio Traffic Reports

Who overturned the tractor trailer?
Who overtook the train?
Who rubbernecked on Route 16,
Never turned left on Main?
Who overran the road divider?
Who missed the overpass?
Who talked back to the traffic cop,
Then stalled, having run out of gas?

*Lillian Morrison*

# 5.
# TRANS
# &
# SUBWAYS

## Song of the Train

Clickety-clack,
Wheels on the track,
This is the way
They begin the attack:
Click-ety-clack,
Click-ety-clack,
Click-ety, *clack*-ety,
Click-ety
Clack.

Clickety-clack,
Over the crack,
Faster and faster
The song of the track:
Clickety-clack,
Clickety-clack,
Clickety, clackety,
*Clackety*
Clack.

Riding in front,
Riding in back,
*Everyone* hears
The song of the track:
Clickety-clack,
Clickety-clack,
Clickety, *clickety*,
Clackety
*Clack.*

*David McCord*

# The Train Melody

The train keeps on
with its chug chug song,
and on it is me
with my own melody:
    river      house      tree
    flower      fence      fisherman
    river      house      tree.
All these are in
my train melody.

Someone waves
and I wave back,
and the train chugs on
down the track
chug chug chug
and on it is me
with my own melody
    flower      fence      fisherman
    river      house      tree.

*Charlotte Zolotow*

## *Travel*

••••••••••••••••••••••••••••••••••••••••••••••••••••••••••••••

The railroad track is miles away,
   And the day is loud with voices speaking,
Yet there isn't a train goes by all day
   But I hear its whistle shrieking.

All night there isn't a train goes by,
   Though the night is still for sleep and dreaming,
But I see its cinders red on the sky,
   And hear its engine steaming.

My heart is warm with the friends I make,
   And better friends I'll not be knowing,
Yet there isn't a train I wouldn't take,
   No matter where it's going.

*Edna St. Vincent Millay*

## *Where Are You Now?*

You are not on the ocean and not in the air,
You are taking a journey and going somewhere.
With a green plush cushion supporting your back
You are traveling smoothly along a bright track,
And everything's moving and slipping and sliding
And going and coming and nothing colliding;
With green fields and meadows and clouds on the hills
And stations and houses and automobiles
And barnyards and pastures and old rusty plows
And rivers and bridges and horses and cows
And children in swimming and clouds in the sky
Coming to meet you and saying good-bye.

*Mary Britton Miller*

## Sing a Song of Subways

········································

Sing a song of subways,
Never see the sun;
Four-and-twenty people
In room for one.

When the doors are opened—
Everybody run.

*Eve Merriam*

## Subway Train

Here come tiger down the track

ROAR—O

Big white eye and a mile-long back

ROAR—O

Through the darkest cave he run

ROAR—O

Never see the sky or sun

ROAR—O

*Lillian Morrison*

## *Flying Uptown Backwards*

Squeezing round a bend, train shrieks
Like chalk on gritty blackboards.

People talk or read or stare.
Street names pass like flashcards.

Hope this train keeps going on
Flying uptown backwards.

*X. J. Kennedy*

# Index of Authors

# Index of Titles

# *Index of First Lines*

j811.54   Roll along.
ROL

$11.95